This book belongs to:

Anna 😊

SCOOBY-DOO!™

The Race Car Monster

By Gail Herman

Illustrated by Duendes del Sur

ADVANCE PUBLISHERS

SCOOBY-DOO!

READ & SOLVE

Find These Fun Activities Inside!

Check the inside back cover for fun things to do!

Bonus story-related activity strips throughout the 15 volumes.

The Swamp Witch

Create your own mystery book,
Scooby-Doo The Swamp Witch!
Color, collect, and staple the coloring pages
at the end of the first 12 books in
the Scooby-Doo Read & Solve mystery series.

Advance
PUBLISHERS

www.advancepublishers.com
Produced by Judy O Productions, Inc.
Designed by SunDried Penguin Design
All rights reserved.
Printed in China

CAR RACE

"Here's a spot!"
Fred pulled the Mystery Machine
into a parking lot.
"Everybody ready to see car racing?"

COUNTING MYSTERY

How many times
does Velma appear
in this book?

"It might rain." Velma said. "And there's no roof over the seats."

"And no snacks!" Shaggy added.

"Ro racks?" said Scooby-Doo. "Ro ray!"

Fred waved a piece of paper. "But I got information in the mail. And free tickets!"

Just then a hot dog cart rolled by. Free tickets? Hot dogs?

"Like, what are we waiting for?" asked Shaggy.

Suddenly the two buddies jumped back in the van.
Shaggy's teeth chattered.
Scooby's fur stood on end.

"W-w-w-we saw something!" said Shaggy.

"What?" asked Velma.

"A riant! Rig, rhite reeth!" said Scooby.

"A giant?" asked Velma. "With big white teeth?"

Everyone looked around.
But nothing was there.
"Are you sure about this?"
asked Velma. "Maybe you made
a mistake."

9

"Hot dogs! Get your hot dogs. French fries! Jumbo size!" the hot dog guy called. Scooby sniffed. "Rummy!"

"Like, maybe we did make a mistake," said Shaggy.

A few minutes later,
the gang sat in their seats.

"Great seats," said Shaggy.

"The first race is about to start,"
said Daphne.

A man stood at the starting line.
He waved a flag, and the cars took off.

"Wow," said Fred. "Those drivers really go!" The cars raced around the track, then passed the gang again.

"Check out those squealing tires!" said Shaggy.

"Rokay," said Scooby. He leaned over the railing.

"Not so far, good buddy," Shaggy said.

All of a sudden, an engine backfired. Shaggy and Scooby jumped in fright — right over the railing!

Thud! They fell onto a speeding car.

"Hang on!" cried Shaggy.

"Ruh-roh," Scooby cried. There it was again. White flashing teeth. Big bloodshot eyes. It *was* a monster!

The car zoomed past.

Rrrrrr! The monster roared.

Frightened, Shaggy and Scooby shot up in the air.

Thud! They dropped back into their seats.

Find two checkered flags on this page, and then find three more on the following pages.

"Stop clowning around," Fred said. "I'm trying to watch the race."

"Ronster!" cried Scooby.

"We saw that thing again," Shaggy gasped. "And it really is a monster!"

"Sure, guys," said Fred. He was watching the race. "Whatever you say."

"Did you hear us, Velma? Daphne?"

"Go, cars, go!" they shouted, excited.

Scooby and Shaggy slumped in their seats. Nobody was listening.

Then the race was over.

"Did you say something?" asked Velma.

"We saw the monster again!" Shaggy cried.

"Why didn't you say so?" asked Fred. "Let's investigate!"

Velma nodded. "Let's start in the parking lot.
That's where Shaggy and Scooby saw the monster."
"I'm not going near that parking lot," said Shaggy.
"Re either," Scooby said.

"Come on, guys," said Fred.

Shaggy and Scooby shook their heads.

"Please?" asked Daphne.

They shook their heads harder.

"We have Scooby Snacks in the van," said Velma.

"And the van is in the parking lot."

Everyone hurried to the van. Velma started
throwing things out of the back.

"I have those Snacks somewhere," said Velma.
All at once, a roar thundered through the lot.

Everyone tumbled into the van.
Crunch! Scooby landed on the Scooby Snacks.
"Yum! Scooby crumbs!" said Shaggy, digging in.

RRRRRR! The monster reared up in front of the gang.

"Zoinks!" cried Shaggy.

It stood as high as the treetops. Sharp teeth flashed.

Find the difference between the Mystery Machine in the story and the one below.

Answer: pink flowers in front and on wheels, colors of Mystery Machine swapped

"Let's get out of here!"

The Mystery Machine took off. But the monster was right behind . . . chasing them . . . getting closer!

All at once, more monsters appeared. Dozens of monsters. All different colors. All different shapes.

27

"I'm driving onto the racetrack," Fred cried.
"It's the only place to go!"
Velma saw the stands.
People were cheering. Jinkies, she thought, that's strange.

28

MYSTERY MIX-UP?

Unscramble the letters to solve these word mysteries.

emtyrys

cmnaehi

krpiagn

rtcuk

tcrrcakae

omtsrne

Then she had an idea. She grabbed the information about the racetrack.

"Like, now you're reading?" said Shaggy. "When there are monsters chasing us?"

"They're monsters all right," said Velma. "Monster trucks!"

Velma showed everyone
the racing schedule.
"Second race: Monster trucks."
Just then they crossed the finish line.
Fred braked. Everyone got out of the van.
"See?" asked Velma. "Those trucks are made
up to look like monsters. Teeth and all!"

A man came up to them, holding a trophy.
"Congratulations!" he said.
"Re ron!" said Scooby.
"Like, cool!" said Shaggy. "And we weren't even trying!"
"Scooby-Dooby Doo!"

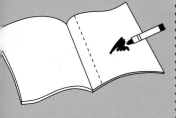

Create your own bonus book!

Step 1:
Color both sides of this storybook page.

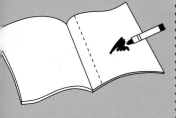

Step 2:
With an adult's supervision, carefully cut along the dotted line.

Step 3:
Repeat steps 1 and 2 in the first 12 books of the Scooby-Doo Read & Solve mystery series.

Please turn page over for further instructions.

"Rook!" cried Scooby.
"Zoinks! Zombie!" cried Shaggy.

Step 4:
Put all 12 cut-out pages neatly in order.

Step 5:
Staple three times on the left side of the paper stack to create the book's spine.

Step 6:
Congratulations, you have solved the mystery!

You have now created your very own Scooby-Doo storybook!